D1387867

Published by Ladybird Books Ltd
27 Wrights Lane London W8 5TZ
A Penguin Company
7 9 10 8 6
© Ladybird Books Ltd MCMXCIX

LADYBIRD and the device of a Ladybird are
trademarks of Ladybird Books Ltd

© Disney MCMXCIX

Based on the Pooh stories by A A Milne
(copyright The Pooh Properties Trust)

Printed in Italy

Disney's

Winnie the Pooh

and the blustery day

It was a blustery day in the Hundred Acre Wood. Winnie the Pooh was strolling towards his Thoughtful Spot. This was his special place for sitting and thinking.

As Pooh walked along, he made up a special blustery day hum about the wind blowing through the leaves on the trees.

When Pooh arrived at his Thoughtful Spot, he sat down on a log.

"Think, think, think," he said, tapping his head. Then, suddenly, Pooh did have a thought. "Why, it's *Windsday*!" he cried. "This is my favourite day for visiting people. I shall start with my dear friend, Piglet."

Now, Piglet lived in a grand old house in a large beech tree. When Pooh arrived, Piglet was sweeping leaves away from the front door.

"I don't mind the leaves that are *leaving*, it's the leaves that are *coming* that bother me," he said to Pooh.

"Happy Windsday, Piglet!" said Pooh, but before Piglet had time to reply…

A gust of wind blew very hard and lifted Piglet up into the air.

"Help me, Pooh!" he cried.

Pooh tried to grab Piglet but all he caught was the end of his scarf. It started to unravel like a ball of string.

"Oh, my!" cried Pooh, "Piglet's flying like a kite!" He held on to the end of the scarf and tried to keep up with his friend.

As they raced along, Pooh passed straight through Eeyore's house and Rabbit's carrot patch.

"Happy Windsday, Eeyore! Happy Windsday, Rabbit!" shouted Pooh. Then, an even bigger gust of wind lifted Pooh right off the ground too.

The wind blew so hard that Pooh
and Piglet landed with a crash against
the door in Owl's treetop house.

Owl was woken from a peaceful
snooze by the loud noise. He
couldn't believe his eyes when he
saw his friends' faces pressed against
the window!

"This is a surprise!" Owl said.
"Do come in for a cup of tea."

He opened the door and Pooh and
Piglet blew in.

"Happy Windsday, Owl!" said Pooh.

While Owl chatted to his friends, the wind shook his house backwards and forwards. Then, all of a sudden, the wind blew *very* hard. The house crashed to the ground with Owl, Pooh and Piglet inside!

Luckily, no one was hurt but the house was in a terrible mess.

Christopher Robin and Pooh's other friends came running over to help.

"I don't think we will ever be able to fix it," said Christopher Robin, shaking his head sadly.

"You'll be needing another house, Owl," said Eeyore. "It might take a day or two, but I'll find one." And Eeyore went off to begin his search.

The very blustery day turned into a very blustery night. Outside Pooh's house it rained and rained and rained. By morning, nearly all of the Hundred Acre Wood was flooded.

When Pooh woke up, he found his honey pots floating in the water. As Pooh got dressed, he decided that it would be a good idea to eat some honey before it all floated away!

Pooh was licking out the honey at the very bottom of a pot when he realised that his head was stuck! Before he could free himself, Pooh began bobbing in the water. He floated right out of the door with his head in the pot and his legs sticking up in the air!

At Piglet's house the water was
coming in through the window. He
had just written a note that read,
"HELP! P-P-PIGLET, (ME)."

HELP!
P-P-PIGLET,
(ME).

He put the note in a bottle. The
bottle floated out of the window and
out of sight. Piglet clung to a chair.
But very soon *he* floated out of the
window and out of sight too!

Now, Christopher Robin lived on a hill where the water could not reach. Everyone made their way to his house to shelter from the flood.

Owl was up in a tree keeping watch.
He saw Rabbit, Kanga and Roo
arrive in an umbrella which Tigger
was paddling. But there was no sign
of Pooh or Piglet.

Suddenly, Roo spotted the floating
bottle with Piglet's note inside.
Christopher Robin read the note out
loud. When Owl heard that Piglet
needed help, he flew off into the
wood to search for him.

As Owl flew over the wood he spotted Pooh and Piglet floating along in the water. They were heading towards a *huge* waterfall!

Piglet disappeared in a gush of water. "Hold on Piglet, I'm right behind you!" cried Pooh.

Minutes later, a very wet Pooh and Piglet appeared on the other side of the waterfall. They floated towards Christopher Robin's house – now Pooh was sitting on the chair and Piglet was stuck in the honey pot!

All Pooh and Piglet's friends were waiting at the edge of the water to greet them as they drifted in.

"Well done, Pooh Bear!" said
Christopher Robin, giving Pooh
a big hug. "You've rescued Piglet.
You're a hero!"

"I am?" said Pooh.

"You are!" Christopher Robin told
him. "And as soon as the flood is
over, I will give you a hero's party."

And so, when at last the Hundred Acre Wood had dried out, everyone joined in the hero's party. Everyone except for Eeyore that is. He was still searching for a new home for Owl.

At last, Eeyore appeared. "I've found Owl a house," he said. "Follow me."

Christopher Robin, Tigger, Piglet,
Pooh, Owl, Rabbit, Kanga and Roo
followed Eeyore through the Hundred
Acre Wood. Eeyore led them to
Piglet's house in the beech tree.

He stood in front of Piglet's front
door and asked everyone to take a
good look at Owl's new home.

No one said a word.

"Well…" said Christopher Robin, at last. "This *would* make a perfect house for Owl."

Everyone turned to look at Piglet.

Piglet looked at his beautiful house and gulped. And then he did a very kind and noble thing.

"Yes," he said, "this is *just* the house for Owl. I hope he will be very happy in it."

Pooh looked at his little friend and
whispered in his ear, "That *was* a
noble thing to do."

Then Pooh said, "Piglet, you can come and live with me."

Piglet accepted at once. "Thank you, Pooh," he said, happily.

So, Christopher Robin gave a party
for two heroes. Pooh was a hero for
saving Piglet's life and Piglet was a
hero for giving Owl a new home.

Pooh and all his friends had a
wonderful time at the heroes' party.
The blustery day hadn't turned out to
be quite so bad after all!